T0197386

Eileen Dover's Fallen Over

Written and Illustrated
by Michelle Hewitt

To order additional copies of this book, contact:
Xlibris
UK TFN: 0800 0148620 (Toll Free inside the UK)
UK Local: 02036 956328 (+44 20 3695 6328 from
outside the UK)
www.xlibrispublishing.co.uk
Orders@ Xlibrispublishing.co.uk

ISBN: Softcover   978-1-6641-1286-5
        EBook   978-1-6641-1287-2

Print information available on the last page

Rev. date: 10/12/2020

Eileen Dover was having a lovely morning, wondering what would happen today. The sun was shining, and she was in a good mood.

She looked out of the window of her little cottage sighing with delight at the little flower heads bobbing prettily in her garden.

When a dragon walked past her front hedge.

"A Dragon?!!" she exclaimed.

Eileen Dover squinted but it definitely looked like a dragon.

She leaned out of her window for a better look.

"Oh no, Eileen Dover's Fallen Over" cried her neighbour as the unfortunate Eileen fell with a thump onto her flower bed.

"Whatever were you doing leaning so far out of your window?" asked her neighbour Betty. "I saw a .a..a dragon walking past the hedge ' spluttered Eileen Dover. "A What?!" exclaimed Betty as she helped Eileen Dover back to her feet.

Together they cautiously peered out of the front gate but there was no dragon to be seen.

Betty took her back indoors and made her a nice cup of tea and after placing a plateful of biscuits in front of Eileen, left saying that she had some important errands to run.

Eileen sighed and helped herself to another custard cream, "looks as though Betty has forgotten what day it is" she mumbled to herself.

Later that morning, she ventured another look out of the window and there walking past her front hedge was an enormous purple bear!

"Oh my" she cried, taking a frightened step back and tripping over the cat who was enjoying a nap in the sunlight streaming in from the window.

"Oh No, Eileen Dover's Fallen Over" barked the dog as he laughed at the poor cat who was currently half squashed under Eileen Dover's leg.

After more calming tea and biscuits, "this really wasn't going to be a good day for dieting" Eileen Dover decided that a calming walk around the village would be a good idea.

She put on her shoes, collected her handbag and walked bravely out of the front door. She checked both directions at the gate in case there were any more strange creatures around but finding the coast quite clear, off she went.

She was walking along thinking about the strange morning when "whump!" she bumped into a tree and was knocked backwards falling onto her bottom

"Oh No Eileen Dover's Fallen Over" some kids nearby cried.

They stopped playing football and helped her back on her feet. She thanked them politely and feeling a little foolish she pulled a couple of twigs from her hair and carried on walking.

She was about to head for home when she saw a procession and there at the front, no she couldn't believe it, it couldn't be, could it?

For there, walking at the head of the crowd was the Queen!

"Impossible" thought Eileen Dover but she peered again and, sure enough, as she squinted, she could make out someone wearing a crown seated on a chair, which was being carried by servants.

Eileen Dover was so excited she hurried to follow them and was amazed to find that the group were heading towards the same road as Eileen's little cottage.

"How thrilling" she breathed, all thought of dragons and giant purple bears forgotten about.

Imagine her great surprise then at the Queen and her party walking straight down her neighbour's path and disappearing into Betty's house.

Eileen Dover didn't quite know what to do. This was incredible. The Queen visiting her best friend and neighbour and not telling her about it. Eileen was so upset. Another cup of tea and the remaining custard creams did little to calm her down and she continued to wonder why her friend had not told her that royalty was coming to visit, "and on my special day too" thought Eileen Dover sulkily.

After finishing her tea, Eileen Dover must have dosed off as she woken suddenly by loud noises coming from her neighbour's back garden.

Eileen Dover couldn't resist the temptation to have a peek over the fence to see what was happening. She fetched her stepping stool and placed it next to the fence. Then she carefully climbed up and peeped over.

The garden was full of people. There were balloons and multicoloured bunting strung between the trees. There were tables ladened with food and drink.

"Surprise!" they shouted.

Eileen Dover was so shocked she (well I'm sure you know) she toppled off the stool and fell right into Betty's garden.

"Oh no Elieen Dover's Fallen Over" the crowd chanted and rushed over to pick her up.

After making sure she was OK all the guests came up to wish Eileen Dover a happy birthday and on seeing them all up close she realised that they were all her friends and family.

"Happy Birthday" they all chorused

"I've had such an odd day" she confessed.

"I saw a dragon walk past my hedge this morning and a huge purple bear, and where is the Queen?" she asked Betty. I saw her wearing a crown and sitting on a throne being carried through the village.

"Hmm..." said her friend Dr Smart
"Can you describe the dragon Eileen?"

The others chuckled but gathered round to listen as Eileen described the blue head and long pointed blue nose, its brown body and the multicoloured pointed spines sticking out of its back and along its very long tail.

"What about the bear?" he asked.

Eileen described its fat body chubby arms and legs and how it had seemed to float past the hedge almost as it if was weightless.

"Interesting" said Dr Smart " And the procession, tell me exactly what you saw there"

Eileen described a line of people following the Queen who was sitting on a throne and wearing a huge crown which was red and trimmed with white fur and had many spikes.

She confessed that "she couldn't actually see the Queen for all the people carrying the throne but she did see someone wearing the crown so that must have been the Queen mustn't it?"

"And I understand you also fell over on the village green too" said Dr Smart kindly.

"Erm, yes mumbled Eileen Dover embarrassed, "I erm, well, I didn't see the tree until I bumped right into it" she added hotly.

Just then the people in front of Eileen Dover moved and there, in the garden, not 20 feet away was a multicoloured unicorn ....

Eileen Dover toppled backwards in her chair in surprise.

"Oh No Eileen Dover's Fallen Over!" they cried once more.

Once upright again she pointed to the unicorn, "Its over there, can't you see it?" she cried

She blinked round the rest of the garden then shouted as she caught a glimpse of the dragon's tail whipping round the trees.

She blinked again and looking in another direction saw the purple bear hovering 6 foot off the floor

"Oh my" she exclaimed and sat back down quickly clutching her chest and thinking she may faint away with fright.

Dr Smart who had followed Eileen's gaze round the garden stood up with a loudly exclaimed "Ah ha, I know exactly what the issue is" and without further ado he walked right up to the unicorn and took something small off its back.

He walked back to Eileen smiling and when he reached her, she saw he was holding a small wrapped box.

"I suggest you open my present straight away" he said "seems I was right in thinking you need them"

Still feeling shocked and disorientated by the lack of concern shown by everyone else to the fact that the garden held a dragon, a purple bear, the Queen and a unicorn she concentrated on unwrapping the present.

Inside was a long sturdy case covered with a pretty fabric. She opened it to reveal a pair of spectacles. "put them on" everyone cried, and Eileen Dover did.

What a difference! Eileen Dover looked round the garden and for the first time saw the expressions on all her friends faces.

She saw, not a dragon's tail, but a long string of multicoloured bunting stretching between the trees.

She saw, not a purple bear but lots of balloons all bobbing about together in the breeze.

She saw, not a royal crown, but a huge white birthday cake with a thick red ribbon with 6 tall candles on the top.

She saw, not a unicorn, but a pile of presents neatly stacked on a table.

She found out during the course of the afternoon that the dragons blue head and long nose must have been Fred's cap and its colourful scaly body the bunting trailing behind him as he walked past to get to Betty's house ready for the party.

The balloons had been walked past Eileen Dover's hedge by little Jemima Fidget who had spent the morning helping to blow them all up to take to Betty's house.

The Royal procession turned out to be Mrs Wilks carrying the cake high in her arms whilst surrounded by her helpful offspring who were bringing extra chairs to Betty's house ready for the party.

"Oh, silly me" she exclaimed "all this time all I needed was a pair of spectacles, now everything is in focus, I will never bump into anything or fall over again"

"We don't believe that" everyone chorused good naturedly and Eileen Dover laughed and helped herself to a large piece of cake.

We hope you have enjoyed this story.

Eileen has some puzzles she would like you to help her with but before you start, check with an adult that you have permission to draw on the book.

It might be a good idea to photocopy the pages and draw on the copies to ensure your book stays in perfect condition.

Join the dots to find the picture is and then colour it in.

Eileen has lost her spectacles, help her get through the maze to fnd them.

Colour in the picture of and find the 12 hidden balloons.

Help Eileen find the hidden words.

```
a   n   f   a   l   l   u   c   w   s
q   d   r   a   g   o   n   d   p   n
r   i   n   p   o   y   i   r   r   a
s   p   e   c   t   a   c   l   e   s
d   a   k   w   z   s   o   r   s   b
c   r   y   b   m   q   r   f   e   i
f   t   o   a   r   u   n   v   n   r
t   y   r   l   t   e   u   o   t   t
u   v   u   l   d   e   c   g   s   h
g   c   r   o   w   n   a   e   b   d
b   d   f   o   p   h   k   u   o   a
i   j   h   n   s   l   e   l   u   y
s   a   b   s   n   b   e   a   r   l
```

Balloons	Crown	Presents
Bear	Dragon	Queen
Birthday	Fall	Spectacles
Cake	Party	Unicorn

Eileen Finger Puppet

With adult supervision, cut out Eileen carefully along with the two finger holes. Turn your fingers into Eileen's legs.

Will Eileen Dover fall over?

Printed in the United States
By Bookmasters